THIS BLOOMSBURY BOOK

BELONGS TO

. . . .

For Nicole

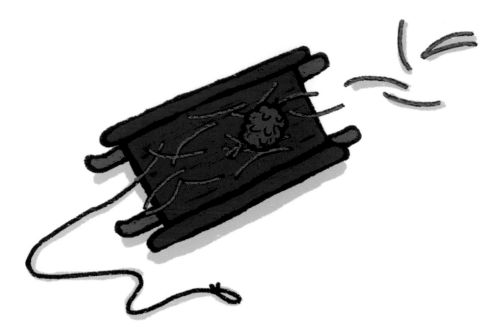

Bloomsbury Publishing, London, New Delhi, New York and Sydney

First published in Great Britain in 2012 by Bloomsbury Publishing Plc
50 Bedford Square, London, WC1B 3DP

Text and illustrations copyright © Salina Yoon 2012

The moral right of the author/illustrator has been asserted

A CIP catalogue record for this book is available from the British Library

HB ISBN 978 1 4088 2881 6
PB ISBN 978 1 4088 2905 9

Printed in China by Hung Hing Printing (China) Co., Ltd., Shenzhen, Guangdong

1 3 5 7 9 10 8 6 4 2

www.bloomsbury.com/childrens

Penguin and Pinecone

a friendship story

Salina Yoon

BLOOMSBURY

LONDON NEW DELHI NEW YORK SYDNEY

One day, Penguin found
a curious object.

It was too brown to be a snowball . . .

too hard to be food . . .

and too prickly to be an egg.

'Whatever you are, you're COLD!'

Penguin got busy.

Penguin loved his new friend.

'What's wrong with my friend?' Penguin asked.

'It's too cold here,' said Grandpa. 'Pinecone belongs in the forest far, far away. He can't grow big and strong on the ice.'

Penguin sighed. 'I'd better take you home, Pinecone.'

Penguin packed his sledge
for the long journey.

The wind pushed hard . . .

but Penguin pulled harder.

Finally . . .

'The forest! Pinecone . . .
you're HOME!'

Penguin made a cosy
nest out of the softest pine
needles he could find.

The day grew hotter and hotter.

'Goodbye, Pinecone. You will always be in my heart.'

Had Pinecone grown big
and strong, just like Penguin?

Penguin set off to find out.

'PINECONE!'

Penguin and Pinecone played and played.

Pinecone was sad to see Penguin go,
but the forest is no place for a penguin.

Penguin and Pinecone may have been far apart . . .

but they always stayed in each other's hearts.

When you give love . . .

. . . it grows and grows.